Longer

The Gold-Threaded Dress

❧ The Gold-Threaded Dress ❧

CAROLYN MARSDEN

SCHOLASTIC INC.

New York Toronto London Auckland Sydney
Mexico City New Delhi Hong Kong Buenos Aires

I would like to thank Panratt Manoorasada, my husband,
for his contributions of Thai culture, and Amy Ehrlich, my editor,
for her guidance in writing this book.

ISBN 0-439-72754-5

12 11 10 9 8 7 6 5 4 3 2 1   5 6 7 8 9 0/0

Printed in the U.S.A.   40

First Scholastic printing, February 2005

This book was typeset in Giovanni.

To my daughters, Preeyanutt Manita
and Maleeka Vayna,
and for my loving husband, Panratt.

C. M.

Chapter One

"Chinese, Japanese." Frankie pulled at the edges of his eyes so they looked like slits. "Americanese!" He let his eyes spring back to normal.

"I am *not* Chinese!" Oy wanted to say. But she just shook her head slightly. She put her hands over the picture she'd been drawing.

Miss Elsa had her back turned, helping other children clean out the hamster cage. Liliandra was holding the straw-colored hamster, Butterscotch. She transferred him from one bent elbow to the other as he tried to scratch her with his tiny claws.

Oy hoped that one day Miss Elsa would allow *her* to hold Butterscotch, but she'd never asked. Other children always seemed to crowd around the cage first.

Frankie teased Oy when Miss Elsa wasn't looking. Because she was new, Oy didn't know whether to talk to her teacher about this or not. Maybe it wasn't serious. Maybe being thought Chinese wasn't a bad thing even though Frankie was trying to make her think so.

"Then what are you?" asked Frankie, putting both hands in his pockets, where he kept his special trading cards.

She was about to say: *Thai. From Thailand. A country near China, but not China. A country with elephants and green jungle.* But Frankie was already talking to Santiago instead.

Miss Elsa turned around. Oy uncovered her picture. It showed her family. But instead of giving them straight black hair and almond-shaped eyes, she'd chosen the brown crayon for the hair and had made the eyes round as coins.

At her old school, no one had said anything to her about being Asian. But since her family had moved across town and she had to go to fourth grade in a new school after the year had begun, this boy Frankie was already bothering her.

"What are you drawing?" Frankie continued. "It couldn't be you and your family. They're all Chinese. Those people look Mexican."

Mexican? She was trying to make them look American. She glanced up at Frankie's eyes. If only she had eyes like all the others, Frankie wouldn't be teasing her.

Because of Frankie, kids on the playground called her *China*, Spanish for Chinese, or sometimes *Chinita*, little Chinese.

Before Oy came from Thailand, she'd looked at pictures of Americans. They had light hair and skin and eyes. When she'd arrived in America though, she saw people of all colors, including very dark ones with black curly hair and even Thai people. Here at school, the children were mostly brown with round eyes.

Just then Liliandra let go of Butterscotch with a squeal. Frankie jumped forward to grab the furry body scampering past his sneakers. When he picked up the hamster, he turned toward Oy. For a moment, it seemed that he would reach out and hand her the soft little animal. But he walked away instead, making a show of stroking and cooing to Butterscotch.

Chapter Two

As Oy walked home, she passed the corner of the playground where Liliandra held secret meetings at recess. A girl had to act cool to be invited to join the club. Oy paused for a moment to study Liliandra's clubhouse, a special spot between the climber and the wall, out of sight of the playground monitors. Would she someday get invited?

Not every girl was in the club. Oy played jump rope and swung on the climber with Kelly Marie who had funny splotches on her skin, and with Marisa who was in the lowest reading group. Sometimes Marisa taught her clapping games: "My mother had a baby, she named him Tiny Tim. . . ." She played with girls from other classes whose names she didn't know. They hardly talked as they played and certainly didn't share delicious secrets like those being whispered in the clubhouse.

When she had told Kun Pa and Kun Mere about the clubhouse, they'd frowned and warned her not to get off track at school. A club wasted time. School was for studying.

Oy stepped around the broken glass on the sidewalk while a brown dog lunged at the chainlink fence.

"I know this neighborhood is not as pretty as Linden Street," Kun Pa had said. "But we have to live with it." Last week, they'd moved to that part of town because rent was cheaper. With less to pay, they could send more money to Oy's Thai Granny, Kun Ya, who still lived in Bangkok.

Oy passed Jerry's Lee Ho Market. She'd seen Frankie go into that store more than once. Probably to buy trading cards. They were forbidden at school but kids brought them anyway, passing them whenever the teachers weren't looking. Sometimes Oy longed to hold the shiny cards and gaze at the magical animals and symbols she saw flash quickly from hand to hand. Her parents would never buy such silly things for her.

At home, she slipped off her backpack, then unfastened her shoes and put them neatly beside the others on the front porch. Her father's shoes were still there — the flip-flops he wore, summer and winter, just like in Thailand. He hadn't gone to work yet.

Inside the kitchen, Kun Mere was still unpacking boxes from the move. "Hello, little daughter," she called. "How was school?" She unwrapped the glasses from their newspaper nests. Her hands were black from the ink.

Kun Pa was lifting Oy's little sister, Luk, up to the faucet to wash her hands. She splashed her fat fingers in the stream of water.

"That boy keeps saying I'm Chinese. Soon everyone in school is going to believe him," Oy announced, shifting from English to Thai.

"That bothers you." Kun Mere turned from the row of glasses on the counter.

"I am not Chinese!"

"People just don't know. They've called me Chinese too," said Kun Pa. He dried Luk's hands.

"Me too," said Luk. She liked to say "Me

too" whenever she had a chance.

"So what did you do about the teasing?" Oy asked.

"I ignored it," said Kun Pa.

"Just tell him you're Thai," said Kun Mere.

"That boy is stubborn. He wouldn't believe me."

"We'll talk more, Oy. Right now," Kun Pa glanced at his watch, "I'm almost late getting back to work."

Oy watched him open the door and slip his feet into his flip-flops. Every day he came home after lunch and returned to work in the evening. Now he would leave the little bit of Thailand they'd created here at home. But soon he'd be in the kitchen at the Royal Thai Buffet, speaking Thai, surrounded by the familiar smells of lemon grass, fish sauce, and *galanka*. Kun Pa still didn't know how it felt to live in the real America.

🪰 Chapter Three

The next day, as the class was going to recess, Liliandra knocked against Oy's backpack so that it fell. Oy turned to see that the photo of herself in her Thai dress had skidded out. Kun Ya had brought the dress from Thailand, and Oy always carried the picture to remind herself of Ya's visit.

Frankie scooped up the photo. "Is this you?" He studied the picture closely, then handed it to Liliandra.

"Oooooh, pretty," said the girls following Liliandra. "Like a princess." Liliandra's eyes opened wide when she saw Oy dressed in pink silk, decorated with jewelry, even a little gold crown.

"That's not even *her* in that dress," insisted Frankie. "It's a trick where they paste the head on a body." But he'd kept the photo longer than anyone.

That afternoon at circle time, Miss Elsa brought the globe down from the shelf. "Boys and girls, let's see where we all come from."

Oy felt her cafeteria lunch of enchilada and beans gurgle in her stomach. She scooted back from the circle until her shoulders hit the bookshelf.

Miss Elsa spun the globe and the United States was hidden. "First, let's see where Rohnan is from." She touched an orange shape with her pencil tip. "Somalia."

Frankie whispered to his friend Santiago behind his hand. They pointed to Rohnan. But everyone already knew that Rohnan was different. He barely spoke English. He didn't play with anyone in the class anyway. Instead, he waited around for his twin brother to come out for recess.

And then it was Hejski's turn. "Finland," Miss Elsa pronounced. But Hejski, despite her name, spoke perfect English and looked so American that she had been the first one invited to become a clubhouse girl. Oy had seen Liliandra and the other girls taking turns combing Hejski's blond hair.

"And now Olivia." Miss Elsa called Oy by her American name, the one her teacher had suggested when, newly arrived from Thailand, she'd entered kindergarten. Even now, when Oy heard "Olivia" she felt as though Miss Elsa were talking about someone else. "Thailand." Miss Elsa's pencil landed again. But Thailand wasn't *purple*! Oy remembered it as green. She wanted to say something, but Frankie hissed "Chinese!" and Santiago pulled his eyes into slits.

Oy relaxed her sweaty fists when Miss Elsa turned the globe in the other direction again. "And," she paused, "here's a country where many of your ancestors came from." This time the pencil hovered over Mexico. *Mexico?* Oy thought about how Frankie had said she'd drawn her family to look Mexican. She looked around, moving only her eyes. Did that mean that these children weren't American either?

"In fact," Miss Elsa continued, "I believe that Valente, who is Native American, is the only one who didn't come from somewhere else."

Valente held his hands over his face and giggled.

Oy understood his embarrassment. She remembered the teacher introducing her on the first day of kindergarten, saying that she'd been born across the ocean. The kids had looked interested but no one had played with her at recess.

"By accident, the picture of me fell out on the ground at school," Oy told Kun Mere that night as she shook out the eating mat and spread it on the floor. "They said that the picture wasn't me. That it was a trick." The table and chairs that came with the house were pushed to the side of the room. Oy wished she could set a place for Kun Pa too, but as usual, he was at the restaurant.

"I hope all this isn't taking away from your schoolwork," said Kun Mere, handing her a shiny aluminum bowl of rice.

Oy set the rice down in the center of the mat.

Luk scrambled toward it, and, before she could be stopped, grabbed a handful.

"You're there to learn, not to teach ignorant little boys," Kun Mere added.

But she *was* learning, Oy thought to herself. More than Mere thought. Exactly what, though, she couldn't put into words.

"Another thing, Mere. Today Miss Elsa told us that most of our class are Mexicans."

"Yes, in this neighborhood that's true."

"Then they're not American either."

Kun Mere laughed and poured chopped vegetables into a sizzling pan. "Oh yes, they're American. Americans come from many different countries."

After they'd finished eating the rice and gingery, stir-fried greens, Oy went to the room she shared with Luk. She took out a piece of paper and drew a picture of herself in her Thai dress. She added each piece of jewelry. In Thai, she wrote: "Even though I may become American, I still love this dress." She folded the paper and put it into an envelope.

คุณย่าค่ะ ถึงแม้ว่าหลาน
อาจจะอยู่แบบอเมริกัน
แต่ยังรักชุดไทย

Oy wrote her Thai granny's address, using American letters and then, again, the Thai alphabet. Whenever Kun Ya visited from Thailand, she taught Oy those letters so that Oy knew them almost as well as she knew the American ones. Oy licked several stamps and put them on the corner of the envelope.

"I want Kun Ya to know that I'm still Thai," she told Kun Mere, giving her the letter to put above Luk's reach.

"That you haven't become Chinese?" Mere pulled Oy into her lap and they both laughed.

Oy wished she could tell Mere about the clubhouse and how she longed to be one of the girls who ran quickly to the special spot at recess. But Mere wouldn't understand.

Luk came and pulled at Oy's arm. But the lap was Oy's for now. "Me too," Luk shouted.

Oy didn't move, but leaned back against

Mere. If only she could draw strength from Mere's tight, strong body.

Later on, Oy went to the drawer where she kept the dress in a plastic bag. She lifted it out and slid her fingertips under the plastic, caressing the stiff pink silk. There were three parts to the dress: the tight skirt and two sashes. During Ya's last visit, Oy had asked Ya to help her put on the dress every day. First came the skirt, then Kun Ya would drape the plain, pleated sash over Oy's right shoulder, across her chest and back. The heavy lace sash went on top. Ya would pin both sashes together at Oy's waist.

Now Oy almost never wore the dress. It wasn't to play in or get dirty, but for wearing at ceremonies. Oy wondered if it even fit her anymore.

Next she opened the cardboard box that held the jewelry. She picked up the bracelet for her upper arm. It rested heavily between her fingers, the gold shining in the dim light.

Like a princess, the girls had said.

✿ Chapter Four

Liliandra beckoned to Oy. Oy tried not to hurry, hoping that Liliandra wouldn't notice that her jeans were too short.

"Hey, Olivia. Forget Frankie. I know you're not Chinese. You're from Taiwan." Liliandra twirled the end of her ponytail with her index finger.

Oy longed to say *Not Taiwan. THAILAND. Taiwan is China.* But she didn't want to ruin her chances with Liliandra.

"I've decided to invite you into the club." Liliandra flipped the ponytail over her shoulder.

Oy looked out over the playground in the direction of the clubhouse.

Liliandra held out one of the special trading cards. A purple pony with wings and a necklace of glowing stars looked as though it would leap right off the paper.

Oy reached for the card.

Liliandra pulled it back and tucked it into the pocket of her overalls. "It's just to look at. Not to touch. But if you come to the clubhouse, you can see it again."

"Sure, sometime." Oy looked away. She didn't want to seem disappointed. If Liliandra saw that Oy felt let down, she would be even meaner.

"There's just one thing." Liliandra narrowed her eyes. "That dress you were wearing in the picture. You have to bring it to school. You have to let each one of us try it on."

Let other girls try on the dress Kun Ya had brought all the way from Thailand especially for her? Oy stared at Liliandra's overalls, her worn flannel shirt. Oy imagined the pink silk dragged along the playground. Maybe Liliandra would let her join and then forget about the dress.

But Liliandra seemed to guess her thoughts. "Before you get into the clubhouse, you bring the outfit."

Oy pushed a little rock with her toe. "I've got to ask my mom."

"Ask your mom? You have to ask your

mom about something like that? It's your dress, isn't it?"

"It's put away somewhere. I'll have to find it."

"Look for it. Bring it Monday. At the club-house I'll tell you a secret about Frankie."

During midmorning recess and lunch recess, Oy played with Marisa, one end of the jump rope tied to a tree. "Teddy Bear, Teddy Bear, turn around. . . ."

Neither Liliandra nor the clubhouse girls paid the slightest bit of attention to Oy. It was as though Liliandra had told her she would never ever be in the club. Oy tried not to let her eyes follow Liliandra and the other girls when they disappeared around the corner of the climber.

Instead, she looked across the green field where Frankie ran back and forth with others in a soccer game. At least he couldn't tease her from so far away. Was Liliandra telling the truth? Did Frankie have a secret?

Chapter Five

"What does the sign on that bus say?" Kun Mere asked Oy.

"Winslow Gardens. It's the next bus." If only Kun Mere would learn to drive! At least on Saturdays, they could drop Kun Pa off at work and have the car.

Kun Mere held out a handful of change.

"Oy, pick out the correct amount."

"It's easy, Mere. I'll show you again. A big silver one and the tiny silver one for each of us. Luk rides free."

Every Saturday Oy went to learn Thai dancing from Pak, the woman who owned the auto-parts store across town. Today she waited in the back room while Pak rang up one more sale. Luk toddled along the dusty floor, pulling herself up against the boxes labeled BATTERY CABLES and BRAKE LIGHTS.

"*Sawasdee*," Pak greeted Oy, her hands pressed together and held against her chest. She gave a little bow.

"*Sawasdee*," Oy answered, bowing in return.

Pak turned on the tape player and the sounds of tiny bells filled the storeroom. Oy noticed that a flash of sadness always crossed Pak's face when the music started. The familiar sounds were a reminder of a life left far behind.

At the sight of Pak's face, Oy recalled the story Kun Pa used to tell her at bedtime back in the days when he worked only the lunch shift. When Oy was almost five years old and still lived in Thailand, Mrs. Bonsub came all the way from America looking for a cook for her restaurant. She invited the applicants to cook just one dish—squid curry. In the kitchen, along with the other prospective cooks, Kun Pa took turns watching through the window into the dining room as Mrs. Bonsub slowly sampled each concoction.

"Times had gotten hard in Thailand," he explained to Oy. "Suddenly, money wasn't worth much anymore. In America, I'd be able to make enough to support you and your mother and send some home to Thailand.

"But America was exactly halfway across the world. I'd be away from my mother, my cousins, my sisters, and brothers. I wasn't sure if I wanted to win that cooking contest or lose it."

Mrs. Bonsub had pushed open the double doors into the kitchen, her long red fingernails clicking against the wood. "Buntoon Chaisang, your dish is the tastiest. Can you leave for the States right away?"

Oy pulled herself back from Kun Pa's story. Pak was giving her two red candles, positioning them between her first two fingers. Although the candles weren't lit, Oy pretended they were. She was practicing *Rhumtein*, the candle dance of northern Thailand. Pak talked about Oy performing the dance for the festival of *Loy Krathong*. If so, she would wear the pink dress.

When she performed this dance, Oy would have to hold the candles very carefully and dance smoothly so that the flames would stay lit. She would have to keep smiling even though drops of hot wax fell on her hands.

Chapter Six

On Sunday, Pak picked up Oy and her family except for Kun Pa, who was away cooking, as usual. Oy loved to touch the small gold Buddha that was glued to the dashboard of Pak's white Mercedes-Benz. Luk grabbed at the garland of plastic flowers hanging from the visor.

On her lap, Kun Mere balanced three metal bowls clamped on top of each other.

The top bowl held pineapple curry, the second rice soup, and the bottom one *pad thai* — noodles with peanut sauce.

Oy liked going to the small temple, which was really just a house in a regular neighborhood. It looked nothing like the temples in Thailand, covered with gold and flashing jewels, with Buddhas as big as buildings.

On Sunday mornings, Oy found herself among people who had narrow brown eyes and black hair and silky skin like hers.

One time, Oy had asked Kun Mere why, except for Kun Pa, all the temple members were women. Mere had told her that the women had married American soldiers who were stationed in Thailand during the war in Vietnam and that the soldiers had brought them to America. They were called war brides.

So the children at the temple, all of whom

were either older or younger than Oy, were only half Thai. They had dark brown hair, instead of black, and their eyes ranged from pure Thai to completely round. But still, Oy wished that children like these went to her school. Then she wouldn't be so alone.

Three monks, in their bright orange robes, were already chanting in the living room. Oy stood on the threshold and breathed deeply, absorbing not only the scent of incense that rose from the corners and the fragrant spices from the kitchen, but also the droning sound of the familiar chants. She and Mere knelt with the other women on the mats before the monks. Luk played with Pak's gold bracelet.

Oy tried not to think of anything at all. She listened to the way her breath passed in and out of her chest. She gazed at the golden

Buddha on the platform above—the serene, half-closed eyes, the hands held as though to bless her.

But today, Oy's mind wouldn't grow quiet. She found herself thinking over and over about Liliandra. Maybe the Buddha could arrange things so that Liliandra would forget about the dress and invite Oy to be a member of the club anyway.

The chanting stopped and the monks went into the dining room to eat their lunch. Oy followed Kun Mere into the kitchen. The women chatted in Thai, while the American husbands gathered by the couch and talked together. Oy thought of only those men as American even though Mere had told her that some of their wives were American citizens too.

Every bit of counter space was covered with plates of food. Mrs. Bonsub had brought delicacies flown in from Thailand. Oy's mouth watered at the thought of the jumbo prawns and the *durian*, that luscious soft fruit. But no one could touch the food until the monks in the other room had finished eating.

Mrs. Bonsub came close to Oy. "I hear that you're doing well in school."

"Yes, Mrs. Bonsub. I make good grades." Oy bowed her head a little.

"That's good. I'm sure your parents are very proud of you."

Oy was afraid that if she looked up into Mrs. Bonsub's face, her expression might reveal that in spite of doing well in math and reading, she was unhappy at school. If Mrs. Bonsub knew that she was having such silly problems, she might wonder if Kun Pa had been a good choice for a cook.

❧ Chapter Seven

Liliandra was just finishing breakfast when Oy came into the cafeteria the next morning. Pretending not to see her, Oy got her food and sat down at a table in the corner. But Liliandra came over anyway, sliding her tray onto the table so that it hit Oy's tray and spilled her milk.

"You got that dress in your backpack?"

Oy slipped the paper off her straw. "That dress is too special to bring." She poked the straw into the carton of juice.

"Too special?" Liliandra pretended to be surprised. "Nothing is too special for me. How about if I'm the only one who tries on the dress? No one else."

Oy took a sip of juice.

"Look." Liliandra opened a notebook. "See, on this page I have all the girls' names written down. Some have smiley faces by their names, like Hejski, others sad faces. I haven't decided about you."

Oy saw her name with the blank space behind it. She drank the carton of pineapple juice in one long gulp. If she didn't keep her mouth closed, she might go ahead and tell Liliandra she'd bring the dress after all.

"Guess you don't want to be in the club

then." Liliandra got up with her tray. Then she turned back. She held up a little package of *saladitos*.

Oy loved the delicious dried fruits that melted in your mouth, salty and bitter and sweet at the same time.

"This is my treat today for the clubhouse girls."

Oy looked down at the soggy cereal and cold bagel that everyone got for breakfast. As soon as Liliandra was gone, she took her tray and dumped the food into the garbage.

As recess drew near, the classroom was filled with whispers.

Frankie sat next to Oy as they finished up their math pages. "Before you came this morning, I saw Liliandra inviting lots of girls from our class, and even some from the other class, into her club. She told them they're going to look for sand rubies." He wrote his name on the top of his paper, then looked up at Oy. "I bet she didn't invite *you*."

"Not yet."

"Probably because you're Chinese."

Oy pretended not to hear. She bent close to her page, holding her pencil tightly.

"What's that you're writing?"

"These are Thai letters. This is my name."

อ้อย

"Cool." He leaned closer so that she felt his breath on her arm. "Can you write *my* name like that?"

Oy took the sheet of paper that he pushed toward her. She spelled out *Frankie* with the mysterious-looking letters of the Thai alphabet: *fa fun, ra rua, nor nu, ga gai.*

แฟรคง

"Wow," he said when Oy handed him the paper. "This really looks Chinese."

Oy let her hair fall over her face. She'd seen Chinese writing and the characters looked nothing like Thai writing, but she wouldn't bother telling Frankie that.

Frankie took the paper, folded it carefully, and tucked it into his pocket.

At recess all the girls gathered around Liliandra, even Marisa and Kelly Marie. Now Oy had nobody at all. She watched from the bench by the classroom door as Liliandra directed everyone to kneel down in the sand. They placed a little sand in their palms and sorted through the grains with their fingertips. Every now and then, a girl would shout "I got one!" and Oy would imagine herself finding a tiny, translucent red grain.

Thailand was famous for real rubies. Kun Mere wore a ring with a sparkling red stone surrounded by tiny diamonds. Yet Oy felt as though she would trade all the rubies in Thailand for the chance to hunt sand rubies with these American girls.

After a while, Liliandra called the girls to the clubhouse. They hurried, brushing the sand from their hands on their pants and dresses. A few cradled something in their cupped hands and Oy guessed they'd found the precious sand rubies.

The playground monitor came up to Oy. "All alone today, *mijita*?"

Oy liked the way the monitor called her "little daughter" in Spanish, the way her own mother did in Thai. "I don't feel well."

"Need to see the nurse?"

"No. I'm just lonesome."

"Ai, mija." The monitor gave Oy a little pat on the shoulder, and was gone.

Maybe she could bring the dress just once. She could guard it carefully while Liliandra tried it on.

At the end of the day, when Oy got her backpack out of her cubby, she found a trading card of a gold dolphin swimming in rainbow-colored water. The sprays of water looked like diamonds. The card was pushed to the back of the cubby, put there on purpose.

Oy slid the card into her palm where nobody would see it. She looked around. No one met her eyes. Yet a secret friend had put it there. Holding the card, she felt a thrill of excitement pass through her, as though her heart were jumping through waves like a care-free dolphin.

Chapter Eight

As Oy opened her homework folder, she felt Kun Mere come to stand behind her. She felt Mere peering at the balloons dittoed across the top of the page of math problems. The balloons had no purpose but to make the homework fun to look at. Oy covered the pictures with her hand.

But Kun Mere pushed Oy's hand aside. "Why do you need those? Why not just the numbers? You're too old to have toys drawn all over your work."

If only Mere would learn more about American ways of doing things! She held so stubbornly to how things were done in Thailand. She would never understand about the club and the clubhouse and the horrible situation with the dress.

Mere watched as Oy added up the double columns. "That's all they give you to do?" she commented. "In Thailand, children have much harder work."

Oy suddenly felt like asking Mere why they hadn't stayed in Thailand then. But she treated her parents with respect no matter what. Once on the playground, when she'd heard a girl say, "I hate my mother!" Oy felt as though the sun had fallen out of the sky. She'd turned to the girl, uncertain that she'd heard her right. But the girl looked angry and must have indeed said those unbelievable words. All day the words had marched back into Oy's mind even though she tried to shut them out.

Oy curled deep inside herself as she penciled in the numbers. Certainly, she'd get no help from Mere in solving the problem with Liliandra. It was up to her. Maybe it didn't really matter so much if she sacrificed something precious from Thailand in order to have friends at school.

"I'll have to talk to that teacher of yours about getting you something harder," Mere finally said. "Come, Luk. Don't bother your sister. She's working."

Secretly, inside herself, Oy said "ha ha" as

the kids at school did when they teased each other. Mere could never talk to Miss Elsa because Miss Elsa didn't speak Thai.

Oy closed the homework folder. Glancing toward the open doorway, she went to the drawer where she kept her Thai dress in the plastic bag. With a quick movement, she unzipped her backpack and put the pink bundle inside.

🌿 Chapter Nine

During silent reading the next day, Oy wrote a note: "I have it." She asked Frankie to hand the paper to Liliandra.

He opened the note instead. "Have what?" he asked loudly. "Must be something from China," he said over his shoulder to Liliandra.

Oy watched Liliandra's eyes widen as Frankie gave her the slip of paper.

"What's going on?" Miss Elsa asked.

"Oh, nothing. My book is just boring," Frankie answered.

"Then get another," Miss Elsa said.

Frankie winked at Oy as he went to the bookshelf.

She felt like winking back. Frankie had protected her. That was lucky. She could hardly imagine what her parents would do if she got in trouble at school.

"Where is it?" Liliandra wanted to know when they got out for recess.

"Right here. In my pack."

Liliandra picked up the backpack, un-zipped it, and lifted out the plastic bag with the dress inside. When the sun hit the golden threads running through the pink silk, Lilian-dra and the other girls gasped. Dozens of fin-gers reached out to touch the glittery material.

"Wait," Oy said. "Liliandra promised that only she would try it on. . . ."

But no one heard because Liliandra was bearing the dress away, toward the clubhouse. "You can come too this time, Olivia," she called back over her shoulder.

Oy stood at the edge of the clubhouse. The tiny spot was packed with girls, and Liliandra was in the middle, pulling the dress over her jeans. Oh, if Kun Ya only knew . . .

"It's tearing," someone said, but Liliandra kept going until she had the tight skirt on.

Oy felt as though she were in a nightmare where she tried to reach out, to speak, to run, but was paralyzed.

Marisa was unwinding the inner sash of the dress. "What's this for?"

"A belt?" Hejski asked.

Oy recalled Kun Ya's fingers tenderly wrapping the silk across her shoulder.

"Then where's the top?"

"Where's the jewelry?" Liliandra called.

"You didn't say anything about jewelry," Oy found herself answering as though from deep inside the dream.

"But it's not the same without the little crown."

"You look pretty enough anyway," said Kelly Marie.

"But not as pretty as Oy did in her picture," said Marisa.

Oy thought of herself smiling in the picture. She remembered Ya stepping backward away from her in the backyard, lining her face up in the viewfinder. The camera had clicked and Kun Ya had whispered, "Oh, my beloved beauty . . ."

"I want to put the dress on, now," Hejski said.

"Not yet," said Liliandra. "It doesn't look

right with clothes on underneath." She wiggled out of the dress and then took off her jeans and shirt and put the skirt back on. She wrapped the sashes around her shoulders. "Better."

Oy knew exactly how the silk, scratchy with the gold embroidery, felt against bare skin. She wanted to grab the dress away from all of them and run someplace far away.

"Now me," said Hejski.

"But you've got blonde hair," said Kelly Marie. "No way will you look good in that. Let me."

Oy watched as Liliandra unwrapped the sashes and handed them to Hejski.

If the dress had already torn, it would tear even more after big-boned Hejski forced her way into it.

As Liliandra began to put on her clothes, Hejski slipped out of hers. Other girls began taking off their clothes too, standing in the striped shadow of the climber in only their underwear.

Just then the bell rang. Everyone giggled and shrieked.

"Quick, give it to me," squealed Kelly Marie.

Oy heard a ripping noise. She looked away. Hearing was bad enough. She couldn't bear to see the fragile silk tear.

"What's all the commotion about? What's going on here?" The playground monitor bent down to look under the climber. "Oh my stars, what happened to your clothes?"

Hejski blushed and covered herself with the narrow skirt.

The principal, Mrs. Cervantes, had extra chairs brought in so that all the girls could sit in a long row in front of her. "And now, would someone please tell me what was going on behind the climber?"

No one said a thing. Oy's heart thudded inside her chest. If Kun Mere or Kun Pa could see her now. Not just wasting time in school, but in deep trouble as well.

"Olivia Chaisang, maybe *you* can explain." Mrs. Cervantes looked over the top of her reading glasses.

"It was my dress. They all wanted to try it on." Oy spread her damp hands flat on the knees of her blue jeans.

"And is the playground a dressing room?"

"No, ma'am."

"You girls know you can't be in just underwear on the playground." Mrs. Cervantes looked at them one by one. Some girls hung their heads; others glanced away when the principal's eyes came to their faces.

"I need to notify your parents about this.

Starting with Olivia. Evidently," Mrs. Cervantes said, taking a pad of paper out of the drawer, "although you were fully dressed, you instigated the situation by bringing a fancy dress to school."

"Oh . . ." Oy said. She rose a little from her chair. Her parents could never know about this! "My mother doesn't understand English."

"And your father?"

"He's working now, cooking. This is a busy time in the restaurant, right before lunch."

"Then I'll write a note. Miss Elsa tells me you're a good student and I'm sure you'll do a fair job of translating. Please bring me a note back with your father's signature."

"That's easy for you," Hejski whispered later to Oy as they gathered for circle time. "You can tell your mom the note says anything—

like they're giving you a special award or something."

"Yeah," said Marisa. "She left a message on my parents' answering machine. I'm gonna be restricted for life."

When the last bell rang, Oy went to her cubby and retrieved the dirty bundle that only that morning had been her Thai dancing dress.

In her pocket, she carried Mrs. Cervantes's note. She'd unfolded it many times and had read the harsh black-and-white words. It said that she, Olivia Chaisang, had taken part in inappropriate behavior on the playground. Not only that, she had provoked it. She'd looked up *provoked* in the dictionary. It meant "to stir up." By bringing the dress, she had caused the girls to get into trouble.

When she walked past the clubhouse, she

noticed that yellow caution tape had been wrapped around the side of the climber. The clubhouse was off-limits. It didn't matter to Oy now. She didn't want to be in that stupid club. She didn't want to be one of Liliandra's girls.

Tears blurred the view of the sidewalk in front of her.

As she walked near Jerry's Lee Ho Market, Oy heard someone following her. She turned to see Frankie. She wiped her cheeks with the back of her sleeve.

He caught up with her. "It was that stupid Liliandra's fault, not yours."

"You think so?" Oy said cautiously. She kept her eyes lowered in case they looked red. Frankie might call her a Chinese crybaby or something even meaner.

"Of course. Liliandra has been getting

other kids in trouble ever since kindergarten."

"But it was my dress from home that started the problem."

"Only a Chinese person would think like that." Frankie gave her a little punch on the arm.

Oy giggled in spite of herself.

"Nah. I'm starting to think you're Korean instead."

"Or Japanese." Oy surprised herself with her own joke.

"Hey, yeah. That's it." Frankie waved as he walked up the steps of the market.

He ascended quickly and didn't invite her to follow him. Oy remembered the way that Liliandra had promised to tell her a secret about Frankie. She wondered now what that secret could be.

Chapter Ten

When Oy got home, she looked through the kitchen window to see Mere in the backyard, shaking out the family eating mat. Luk played on the rusty swing set. She watched the two of them, going on with the day as though nothing were wrong. Oy fingered the note in her pocket, ruffling the edges.

She thought of Hejski's advice. Oy could translate the note however she wanted: "PTA Meeting Next Tuesday at 6:30" or "Field Trip to the Zoo Coming Up." She didn't have to show the note to Kun Mere at all. Mere would never know that Mrs. Cervantes had written it. And no one would tell Kun Pa because he was too busy working to ever go to Oy's school.

It would be easy to write a response that looked like Kun Pa's small, neat American writing: "We are very sorry for our daughter's bad actions." Faking his signature would be easy too.

Kun Mere hung the mat over the back of a chair, then turned to push Luk in the swing.

But Oy already felt shame burning inside her like the *nam prik* sauce made of the tiny, fiery chiles Kun Mere grew in the backyard. She couldn't imagine adding more to her shame by lying to her parents.

Oy went into her room. Although everything had changed in just one day, the room still looked the same: her small desk in the corner, the sleeping mat rolled against the wall, a travel poster of Thai fruits pinned up by the window. She stuffed the dress far back in her closet, underneath a quilt stored for the cold season.

"Welcome home, little daughter," Kun Mere called when Oy entered the backyard.

"*Sawasdee*, Kun Mere," Oy greeted her formally, pressing her hands together.

Mere stopped pushing Luk and glanced at Oy. "Is everything all right?"

"No, I have bad news."

Mere left the swing and walked across the dry grass to Oy. Luk protested, crying for more pushes. "What is it, Oy?"

Oy took the note from her pocket and opened it up. The words stood out boldly and clearly in the bright sunshine. To Oy, they shouted their meaning in all languages.

"What does it say, little daughter?" Mere stood close and peered at the paper.

"It says that I caused trouble on the playground."

Mere looked confused. She made a little movement with her hand, as though to take the note, then drew it back. "How?" she finally asked.

Oy sat down on a faded lawn chair. The clear sunshine would expose the truth. "Mere, forgive me."

Kun Mere sat down in a chair next to her. She didn't seem to hear Luk's protests at losing her attention.

"Remember I said that the girls saw the picture of me in the Thai dress?"

Mere nodded, her eyes never leaving Oy's face.

"A girl wanted to try on the dress. She said she wouldn't be my friend if I didn't bring it to school."

Mere screwed up her face as though she were trying to understand.

"I brought the dress. Without your permission." Oy took a deep breath and rushed ahead with the story. "All the girls wanted to try it on. They were so excited they took their clothes off, waiting for their turns."

A little smile played around the edges of Mere's lips.

"The woman who watches the playground caught us. The principal said the disgraceful behavior was my fault."

"Oh, little daughter . . ." Mere looked down into her hands.

Oy glanced at Luk, swinging innocently. Even she would be affected. When she went to school, people might remember that she was the sister of Olivia Chaisang, who had provoked Liliandra's clubhouse girls to inappropriate behavior.

Mrs. Bonsub would find out about this disgrace. She would fire Kun Pa for having such a daughter. With no job for Kun Pa, the whole reason for coming to America would be lost.

"That girl doesn't sound like a good friend," Mere said at last.

Oy thought of the way Liliandra teased and demanded. "No, she isn't nice. She's taken all the girls for her friends. I just want to fit in with them. Oh, Mere." She began to cry, putting her face in her hands. "You don't know how bad it feels to be left out!"

Birds sang in the palm tree overhead. How could their songs be so joyful?

"Oy," Mere said softly, touching Oy's hair, smoothing it around her ears, "I also know how it feels to be different."

Oy suddenly saw Mere in the grocery store, examining the bottles for pictures on the labels, looking for the fermented fish sauce that she would never find. She would stare at unfamiliar vegetables like avocado or artichoke, then turn away from them with a shake of her head. At the checkout stand she would move her hand back and forth in a gesture for *no*, she didn't understand, when someone tried to speak to her in English.

"Oh, Mere . . ."

Like Oy, Kun Mere didn't belong to this country. Now not only was she different from everyone else, but she'd become the mother of a child who had shamed the family name.

Mere leaned forward in the lawn chair. "To

be alone is hard, Oy. But no friend is better than a cruel one."

That was true. Oy didn't want to please Liliandra anymore. But she did want a friend. She thought of the trading card of the dolphin pushed to the back of her cubby. Someone had been kind to her. Neither Marisa nor Kelly Marie had any trading cards. Besides, they never came into her classroom. But Frankie always carried cards in his pocket. His cubby was close to Oy's. Could he have put the card in there?

She sat with Kun Mere as the sun moved behind the palm, casting big, feathery shadows over the backyard. After a while, Luk got down off the swing. She came over and curled up in Mere's lap.

"One more thing, Mere," Oy began quietly. "The dress got ruined."

"Were those American girls too big for it?" Mere asked. Again, Oy noticed a hint of a smile.

"They were big and in a hurry."

"And greedy?"

Oy had to smile too.

"Bring it to me."

When Oy went inside, at first she couldn't see in the dim light. She felt underneath the winter quilt until she found the silk with its scratchy threads.

Mere held the dress up in the sunshine. It was torn on one seam and smudged with playground dirt. Even so, the threads still shone. Mere gently urged Luk off her lap. "Go get the sewing kit from the dresser, Oy."

When Oy came back with the carved wooden box, Mere threaded a needle with pink thread. "Like this, little daughter." She pushed the needle through the fabric, taking tiny stitches. Then she handed the needle to Oy.

While Mere weeded her patch of chiles and lemon grass, with Luk helping her, Oy sewed her Thai dancing dress.

When the seam was mended, Mere filled a tub with cool water. She showed Oy how to wash the dress very gently. "Remember, little daughter," Mere said as they stretched the fabric and hung it in the bathroom to dry, "the children are interested in this dress not because it makes them look the same, but because it makes them look different."

That evening, Kun Pa wrote a note: "Dear Mrs. Cervantes, Thank you for your letter. I appreciate your concern. My daughter needs a friend." He signed it Buntoon Chaisang, in fancy Thai letters:

บันทูล ฉายแสง

❧ Chapter Eleven

The next day at school, everyone was quiet. Liliandra's mother had sent a note saying she was sick with fever. The girls drifted to play in small groups. From the top of the climber, Oy and Marisa looked down at the former clubhouse.

"That place wasn't that much fun after all," said Marisa, dangling her long braids over the bar.

"Not the way she promised," Oy added.

"No. And we waited so long to get invited. Sorry about your dress."

"It wasn't your fault. Anyhow, my mom and I fixed it."

"Liliandra didn't even look good in it." Marisa looked straight at Oy. "Not like a princess like you."

Oy held on to the climbing bar with both hands. "Maybe you could come to my house some day and try it on."

"Oooh, cool." Marisa gave a little jump.

After school, as she was walking home, Oy again noticed Frankie following her.

"What did your parents say?" he asked when he caught up with her.

Oy shielded her eyes from the light to better see his face. Was he teasing her again? "They were okay about it."

Frankie stopped in front of Jerry's Lee Ho Market.

Oy wondered where Frankie got money to buy trading cards every day.

"Want to meet someone?" Frankie asked.

"Where?" Oy glanced around, but they were alone.

"In the market. Don't you know that this place belongs to my family?"

Oy looked with new interest at the tall white walls of the market where sometimes Kun Pa bought fresh vegetables or cooking oil.

"Come inside." Frankie walked up the steps without turning around, as though he knew she'd follow.

Inside, the store was lined with shelves of cans and bottles.

At the back, Oy saw a very old man, his face like a wrinkled moon. When she drew closer, she saw that the man's eyes were narrow, the thinnest of slits in his dry face.

"This is Yeh-Yeh." Frankie's voice was quiet, yet it echoed in the high ceilings. "He's my grandfather. Yeh-Yeh, this is Olivia, a friend of mine from school."

Yeh-Yeh nodded ever so slightly, then walked slowly into the back room.

Oy stared at Frankie. "But he's Chinese."

Frankie nodded.

Oy felt a laugh rise like a bubble in the back of her throat. "Then so are you."

"Not so fast." Frankie held his thumb and forefinger apart about an inch. "Just a little bit. A quarter, to be exact."

"You're the one who's Chinese. Yet you teased me!"

"I'm sorry, Olivia. When I was in kindergarten Yeh-Yeh used to walk me to school. The kids teased me about being Chinese.

When they saw me coming, they pulled their eyes out like this—" Frankie jerked the edges of his eyelids with his fingertips. "They sang a stupid little song: '*Ching, chong, here comes the Chinaman.*'" He brushed the hair off his forehead. "I'm sorry."

"Oh . . ." Oy said, letting her backpack slip off her shoulder. She could almost hear the children singing those awful words.

Frankie suddenly bent down behind the counter. When he stood up, he held out a shiny packet. "For you. To make up for being so mean."

The trading cards felt slippery and magical in her hand. "So it was you." She pulled the gold dolphin card from her pocket.

Frankie blushed. "Yeah, Olivia. That was me. I knew Liliandra was giving you a hard time."

"But you did too."

"I just wanted to be friendly. Especially when I saw your picture. The way you were all dressed in jewels and gold, you looked like you came from somewhere exciting."

"Yeah, Thailand."

"Thailand," Frankie repeated.

Oy shuffled the gold dolphin in with the other cards. She looked back up at Frankie. "Thank you for these."

"It wasn't nothing, Olivia." Frankie took a step toward her. "I can get you more."

"Frankie, just one thing—my name isn't really Olivia. It's Oy."

"Sounds Japanese."

"Oh, you *Chino* . . ." Oy punched Frankie lightly on the shoulder.

"Hey, there!" said Frankie. But he was smiling.